PAUL GALLICO'S
THE SMALL MIRACLE

RETOLD BY
BOB BARTON

ILLUSTRATED BY
CAROLYN CROLL

HENRY HOLT AND COMPANY

NEW YORK

For my grandchildren:
Callum, Emily, and Mallory
—B. B.

For Tomie, Maureen, Kathy,
Luisa, Angelo, and "il gruppo"
—C. C.

Henry Holt and Company, LLC
Publishers since 1866
115 West 18th Street
New York, New York 10011
www.henryholt.com

Library of Congress Cataloging-in-Publication Data
Barton, Bob.
Paul Gallico's The small miracle / retold by Bob Barton ; illustrated by Carolyn Croll.
p. cm.
Summary: When his beloved donkey becomes ill, a young Italian boy is determined
to take her to the crypt of St. Francis in Assisi in hopes of making her well.
[1. Donkeys—Fiction. 2. Italy—Fiction.] I. Title: Small miracle.
II. Gallico, Paul, 1897–1976, Small miracle. III. Croll, Carolyn, ill. IV. Title.
PZ7.B2847 Pau 2003 [E]—dc21 2002010853
ISBN 0-8050-6745-0
First Picture-Book Edition—2003 / Designed by Martha Rago
Printed in the United States of America on acid-free paper. ∞

1 3 5 7 9 10 8 6 4 2

The artist used Arches 140-pound hot-press watercolor paper, Winsor & Newton watercolors,
graphite pencil, and colored pencils to create the illustrations in this book.

ONCE THERE WAS a boy named Pepino who lived in the mountain town of Assisi. He had no mother. He had no father. He lived in a stable with his donkey, Violetta.

Violetta was everything to Pepino. She was mother to him. She was father to him. She was playmate, companion, and comfort. Pepino and Violetta were a familiar sight around Assisi. Together they delivered wood, water, and olives to pay for their food and lodging.

Violetta had a curious expression around the corners of her mouth that made her appear to smile. Pepino's hard work and Violetta's smile brought them lots of jobs and made people happy.

One day Pepino noticed the little donkey was getting slower. Her once well-padded ribs were beginning to show through her sides. She tired easily. Most distressing of all, Violetta had lost her enchanting and lovable smile.

Pepino took Violetta to Dr. Bartoli, who dosed her with medicine.
He tried his best, but the little donkey continued to lose weight. She
grew weaker.

Then Pepino took Violetta to the parish priest.

"The patron saint of our village, Saint Francis, loved all birds and animals, Pepino," the priest said, looking at the sick donkey. "You must pray to Saint Francis to heal Violetta."

As Pepino led Violetta home through the crooked streets of Assisi he had an idea. "I will take Violetta up to the Basilica of Saint Francis. If I can get her to smile again, Saint Francis will want to make her well."

When Pepino reached the basilica, he found the Bishop deep
in conversation with the stonemason.

Suddenly the Bishop noticed Pepino. "Yes, my son?"
"Please, sir, my donkey is very sick. May I take her into the crypt so that Saint Francis can see her? Perhaps he will make her well."

The Bishop looked surprised. "You can't take a four-footed
animal down a winding staircase. Besides, it's barely wide enough
for a human."

Pepino put his arm around Violetta's neck. Tears filled his eyes.

The stonemason stroked his chin. "There is another entrance, sir. It is through the old church. The passage has been walled up, but it could be opened."

"Only His Holiness the Pope can make that decision," said the Bishop. "I'm sure he would be touched by your story. But he is very busy. It would be impossible for you to see him. I'm sorry, son."

Pepino took Violetta back to the stable. He fed and watered her. He asked the stableman what he should do.

The man shook his head slowly. "There is nothing more you can do, Pepino. One must accept things as they are."

Pepino thought and thought. Suddenly he burrowed under the straw and pulled out the jar that held his savings. He stuffed a few lira notes into his pocket, then rubbed Violetta's muzzle a hundred times.

Pepino knew a man who owned a truck. He gave the man some of his lire. Soon they would be in Rome.

In the early morning light of Saint Peter's Square, the barefoot Pepino looked up at the massive dome of the basilica. The size and majesty of the building began to sap his courage. But then he thought of the little donkey with the clouded eyes and heaving flanks who didn't smile anymore.

"Violetta will die unless I find help for her," Pepino said to himself. "What can I do now?"

As Pepino wandered to the side of the building he saw an old woman selling spring flowers. "Saint Francis loved flowers," he thought. "Perhaps the Pope does, too!"

Minutes later, Pepino edged close to a Swiss Guard on duty at the side door to the Vatican. In one hand Pepino held a tiny bouquet of violets. In the other he had a handwritten note.

"Please take these to the Pope," he begged. "When he sees the flowers and reads what I have written, I am sure he will see me."

The astonished guard took the note and read it. For a moment it seemed he would send the boy away, but something about the message and the look on the boy's face had touched his heart. "Wait here," he said.

From the hands of the Swiss Guard the note and flowers were put into the hands of a clerk, who passed them to another. Hand to hand, the note and flowers traveled along corridors and up stairways as each person, touched by the offerings, hurried them on to their final destination.

At last they were placed on the desk of the man for whom they had been intended. The Pope opened the note and read it.

Dear and Most Sacred Holy Father,

These flowers are for you. Please let me see you and tell you about my donkey, Violetta. She is very sick. The Bishop will not let me take her to see Saint Francis so that he may cure her. I live in the town of Assisi. I have come all the way here to see you.

Your loving Pepino

The Pope sat quietly, looking from the note to the flowers. They had begun to lose their freshness, but they had not lost their message of love and hope.

The Pope called his secretary. "Let the child be brought to me. I will see him."

Pepino perched on the edge of his chair and told the Pope about Violetta. "I know if I can take her into the crypt of Saint Francis and get her to smile that Saint Francis will make her well."

The Pope looked thoughtful and then he said, "Pepino, there is something you must understand before a decision can be made. It is your hope that, because of your faith in Saint Francis, he will help and heal Violetta. But had you thought, Pepino, that he who dearly loves and cares for all God's creatures might come to love Violetta so greatly that he would wish her at his side in Eternity?"

Pepino's eyes filled with pain. "No, Your Holiness, I had not thought..."

"Will you go to the crypt only to ask, Pepino, or will you also, if necessary, be prepared to give?"

Pepino raised his stricken face. He looked at the Pope. Something deep within gave him courage.

"I will give . . . if I must, but I hope he will let her stay with me just a little while longer."

At the end of half an hour, Pepino had been given the Pope's blessing. He had also been given a letter to bring to the Bishop, granting permission to break down the wall.

Pepino's heart beat wildly all the way back to Assisi. After
checking on Violetta, he flew through the crooked streets to deliver
the Pope's letter.

Clink, clink, clink rang the stonemason's pick the following morning. Pepino, wide-eyed and pale, stood with his arm around Violetta. Beside him, the parish priest and the Bishop watched while broken bricks and clods of mortar fell from the walled-up doorway leading to the crypt.

Suddenly a large chunk of wall crashed down. More masonry tumbled. Plaster dust swirled. Through a narrow opening Pepino could see the flicker of candles placed at the altar wherein rested the remains of Saint Francis.

"Please, sir, may Violetta and I go into the crypt now?"

"Yes, Pepino," said the Bishop kindly. "You may enter now."

The hooves of the donkey made a sharp *clip clop, clip clop* on the ancient flagstones of the passageway.

Pepino did not support her now. His hand rested lightly and lovingly on her neck as she walked beside him, her head held high.

In the flickering dusty candlelight, the Bishop was certain he saw the little donkey smile as she and the boy moved forward to complete their pilgrimage of faith.